CONTENTS

Mink fur was popular for coats. It is long and dense.

American Minks Invade the United Kingdom

By Susan H. Gray

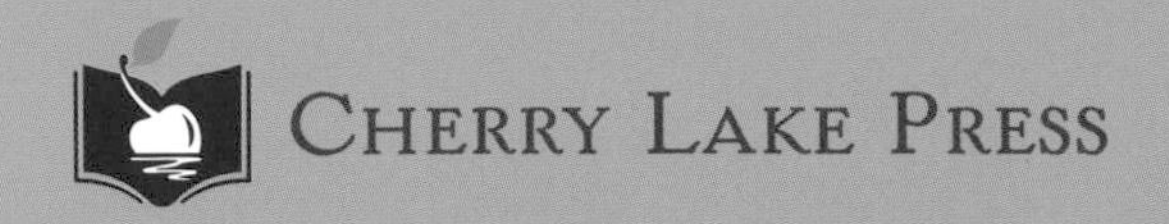

Published in the United States of America by Cherry Lake Publishing Group
Ann Arbor, Michigan
www.cherrylakepublishing.com

Reading Adviser: Beth Walker Gambro, MS, Ed., Reading Consultant, Yorkville, IL
Book Designer: Melinda Millward

Photo Credits: © Stephan Morris/Shutterstock.com, cover, 14; © Gallinago_media/Shutterstock.com, 4; © Film Studio Aves/Shutterstock.com, 6, 20; © Geoffrey Kuchera/Shutterstock.com, 8; © Intothewild_by/Shutterstock.com, 10; © Jelena Safronova/Shutterstock.com, 12; © MikeLane45/iStock.com, 16; © RobinEriksson/iStock.com, 18

Cherry Lake Press is an imprint of Cherry Lake Publishing Group.
Library of Congress Cataloging-in-Publication Data

Names: Gray, Susan Heinrichs, author.
Title: American minks invade the United Kingdom / by Susan H. Gray.
Description: Ann Arbor, Michigan : Cherry Lake Publishing, 2021. | Series: Invasive species science : tracking and controlling | Includes index. | Audience: Grades 2-3
Identifiers: LCCN 2021004928 (print) | LCCN 2021004929 (ebook) | ISBN 9781534187078 (hardcover) | ISBN 9781534188471 (paperback) | ISBN 9781534189874 (pdf) | ISBN 9781534191273 (ebook)
Subjects: LCSH: American mink–Control–Great Britain–Juvenile literature. | Introduced animals–Great Britain–Juvenile literature. | Invasive species–Control–United States–Juvenile literature.
Classification: LCC QL737.C25 G736 2021 (print) | LCC QL737.C25 (ebook) | DDC 599.76/6270941–dc23
LC record available at https://lccn.loc.gov/2021004928
LC ebook record available at https://lccn.loc.gov/2021004929

Cherry Lake Publishing Group would like to acknowledge the work of the Partnership for 21st Century Learning, a Network of Battelle for Kids. Please visit http://www.battelleforkids.org/networks/p21 for more information.

Printed in the United States of America
Corporate Graphics

Get Out!

Simon was fed up. From 1950 to 1960, hundreds of mink farms had sprung up across Europe. They fed an international demand for mink coats, scarves, and hats.

Like most other English fur farmers, Simon had **imported** American minks for his business. At first, Simon made a good living selling his animals.

Minks live partially on land and in water.

But mink farming wasn't as easy as he had thought. Minks need a large, clean place to swim. They are **mammals** that need plenty of meat. They figured out how to escape their enclosures. And now, they had killed two of Simon's chickens. One by one, Simon opened the minks' cages and set them free.

Look!

Find pictures online of American minks and European minks. How are they alike? How are they different?

American minks can have one to eight **kits** at a time.

A Disaster Unfolds

American minks are **native** to the United States and Canada. In the 1920s, farmers imported the first ones into Great Britain. Some minks escaped. Some farmers, like Simon, released theirs on purpose. Before long, mink populations were growing and spreading.

Britain was not the only place where this happened. It occurred in other European countries, as well as Asia and South America.

Minks kill their prey by biting their neck.

Over time, people noticed certain native animals were disappearing. Water **voles**, sea birds, and fish **species** were becoming rare. Studies were done. Finally, it became clear. The American mink was an **invasive** species. It was wiping out birds, voles, and fish. And it was everywhere.

Make a Guess!

It takes years for people to realize that some animals are invasive. Why does it take so long?

Hunting hounds used to hunt minks
can disturb wildlife in their search.

What to Do?

Around 1965, British experts decided that something must be done. The government hired seven trappers to catch and remove the invaders. But by 1970, everyone realized this small effort was getting nowhere.

Over time, many people tried different tactics. Some held hunting trips using hounds to find the minks.

Minks are good at hiding! They reuse abandoned dens.

People also tried widespread trapping. But setting and checking traps takes a lot of time. Someone with 50 traps must check each one every day. Plus, the traps might catch harmless animals instead of minks.

Today, scientists are getting creative. They have started using “smart” traps. They are also studying how to outwit the most **elusive** minks.

Think!

Why should someone check their traps every single day?

Traps are filled with bait to lure in minks.

Smart traps have a built-in messaging system. As soon as an animal enters, the trap door slams shut. The system then sends a text or email to the trap's owner. The notice also includes the trap's identification number. So a trapper no longer wastes time checking empty traps. One or two trappers might be able to oversee hundreds of traps.

Once scientists detect a mink's DNA, they will keep looking until they find it.

Sneaky Minks, Sneakier Scientists

What about timid minks that won't go near a trap? How will anyone find them? Scientists might, by following their DNA.

DNA is a **molecule** in the cells of living things. American mink DNA is different from that of all other animals. Researchers can now find **aquatic** animals' DNA in the water where they swim. Even a shy mink can't hide its DNA!

Minks are able to outsmart predators. With the help of new technology, humans have better luck catching them.

Thanks to new technology, there is now hope. Trappers can work more efficiently. Scientists may find the most elusive animals. They can remove these invaders from the environment. Perhaps one day, the American mink will no longer be a problem.

Ask Questions!

Water voles live at the edges of ditches, streams, and rivers. They eat plants and build burrows. Burrows help to dry the soil. This allows a greater variety of plants to live there. If minks eat all the voles, what happens to the soil and plant life?

GLOSSARY

aquatic (uh-KWAH-tihk) living in or near water

elusive (ee-LOO-sihv) difficult to find; hiding out

imported (im-PORT-ihd) brought in from another place

invasive (in-VAY-sihv) not native, but entering by force or by accident and spreading quickly

kits (KITS) young animal offspring

mammals (MAM-uhlz) animals that have hair and produce milk for their young

molecule (MAHL-uh-kyool) a very small compound made up of atoms

native (NAY-tihv) occurring naturally in a particular place

species (SPEE-sheez) a particular type or kind of plant or animal

voles (VOLZ) small mammals that are part of the rodent family

FIND OUT MORE

BOOKS

Gilles, Renae. *Invasive Species in Infographics*. Ann Arbor, MI: Cherry Lake Publishing, 2020.

Kalman, Bobbie. *Invasive Animal Species*. St. Catharines, ON, Canada: Crabtree Publishing Co., 2016.

WEBSITES

Biokids—American Mink
http://www.biokids.umich.edu/critters/Neovison_vison
Find answers to your questions about the size of minks, their babies, lifespan, and favorite foods.

Britannica Kids—Mink
https://kids.britannica.com/kids/article/mink/390130
Discover more about minks through descriptions, photographs, and videos.

DK Findout! Mink
https://www.dkfindout.com/us/animals-and-nature/weasels/minks
Read interesting facts about minks' behavior and swimming feats.

INDEX

ABOUT THE AUTHOR

Susan H. Gray has a master's degree in zoology. She has written more than 180 reference books for children and especially loves writing about animals. Susan lives in Cabot, Arkansas, with her husband, Michael, and many pets.